The Easter Story

Retold by Russell Punter

Illustrated by John Joven

D0300071

A long time ago, there lived a man named Jesus.

He went across the land, telling people about God's kingdom.

At the city of Jerusalem,
cheering crowds lined the streets.

The day after he arrived, Jesus visited the local Temple.

When he saw traders selling things, he was furious.

"This is a place for praying," he shouted, "not making money."

Jesus chased them away and spoke about God.

Sick people came to hear him
and he made them well.

The Temple priests grew angry.

"Jesus says he's the Son of God," they fumed, "and that's not allowed."

Let's arrest him, away from the crowds.

Judas, one of Jesus's friends, overheard them.
"Pay me, and I'll tell you when Jesus is alone," he whispered.

That night at supper, Jesus shocked his friends.

"The man I give this bread to will betray me," he declared.

Jesus handed the bread to Judas, who ran off.

Jesus murmured a prayer, then shared
a meal with his friends.

"When you eat bread and drink wine, please think of me," he said.

After supper, they walked
to a nearby garden.

"Soon, you'll all run off and leave me," said Jesus.

His friends were heartbroken. "We'd never do that!"

Jesus turned to his friend, Peter.
   "And you'll say you don't know me, three times."

Never!

Jesus made his way to another part of the garden to pray alone.

When he returned, his friends were fast asleep.

Couldn't you stay awake for me?

Suddenly, Judas was there with the Temple guards.

Striding over, he kissed Jesus on the cheek.

"This is the man you want," he told them.

Jesus's friends ran off in fear.

The soldiers marched Jesus to the High Priest's palace.

Peter joined the crowds outside.

Hey, aren't you a friend of Jesus?

Erm, no.

Peter told the same lie twice more.

Then, remembering what Jesus had said, he wept.

The Temple priests asked the Roman Governor,
Pontius Pilate, to kill Jesus.

Pilate thought Jesus was innocent.

But he didn't want
to upset the priests.

Roman soldiers dressed Jesus in purple robes and stuck a crown of thorns on his head.

"Ha! Now you really look like a king!" they jeered.

They dressed Jesus in his old clothes again.

Then they made him drag a huge
wooden cross out of the city.

Before long, Jesus was exhausted.

As a crowd gathered, the soldiers hung Jesus on the cross.

Jesus prayed to God.

"Forgive them, Father.
They don't know what
they're doing."

That afternoon,
Jesus died.

The ground shuddered
and shook.

"He really must have
been the Son of God,"
cried a soldier.

A man named Joseph wrapped Jesus's body in a linen cloth.

Then he took the body
to a garden with some friends...

...and they laid it gently inside a tomb.

Puffing and panting, they heaved a heavy rock
across the entrance.

By now, it was late on Friday evening.

On Sunday, three of Jesus's friends visited the tomb.

To their amazement, the huge rock had been moved.

Jesus's body was gone!

Just then, a man appeared
dressed all in white.

"Don't be afraid," he
called out to them.
"Jesus is alive."

The women ran off
to tell the others.

When a woman named
Mary came back alone,
there stood Jesus.

"Tell my friends you've
seen me," he said.

Jesus's friends saw him several times after that,
before he finally rose up to Heaven.

They told everyone they met the good news...

Jesus would live forever.

The Easter story is nearly two thousand years old. It comes from the section of the Bible known as the New Testament.

Edited by Lesley Sims

First published in 2016 by Usborne Publishing Ltd., Usborne House, 83-85 Saffron Hill,
London EC1N 8RT, England. www.usborne.com Copyright © 2016, 2013 Usborne Publishing Ltd.